For Vijay, Mila, and Indie

BLOOMSBURY CHILDREN'S BOOKS
Bloomsbury Publishing Inc., part of Bloomsbury Publishing Plc
1385 Broadway, New York, NY 10018

BLOOMSBURY, BLOOMSBURY CHILDREN'S BOOKS, and the Diana logo
are trademarks of Bloomsbury Publishing Plc

First published in Great Britain in August 2019 by Bloomsbury Publishing Plc
Published in the United States of America in February 2020
by Bloomsbury Children's Books

Bloomsbury books may be purchased for business or promotional use. For information on bulk purchases please contact
Macmillan Corporate and Premium Sales Department at specialmarkets@macmillan.com

Library of Congress Cataloging-in-Publication Data
available at https://lccn.loc.gov/2019020696
ISBN 978-1-5476-0300-8 (hardcover)
ISBN 978-1-5476-0301-5 (e-book) • ISBN 978-1-5476-0302-2 (e-PDF)

Art created digitally using Kyle T. Webster's natural media brushes for Photoshop and a selection of hand-painted textures
Typeset in Appareo Medium • Book design by Goldy Broad
Printed and bound in China by Leo Paper Products, Heshan, Guangdong
2 4 6 8 10 9 7 5 3 1

All papers used by Bloomsbury Publishing Plc are natural, recyclable products made from wood grown in well-managed
forests. The manufacturing processes conform to the environmental regulations of the country of origin.

To find out more about our authors and books visit www.bloomsbury.com and sign up for our newsletters.

RAVI'S ROAR

TOM PERCIVAL

BLOOMSBURY
CHILDREN'S BOOKS
NEW YORK LONDON OXFORD NEW DELHI SYDNEY

Ravi was the youngest
and the smallest
in his family.

KIRAN

JAYA
ANIL

RAVI

Everyone was bigger than him . . .

. . . even Biscuits the dog!

Most of the time, being the smallest was **great** . . .

. . . but sometimes, just *sometimes*, it wasn't.

One day, Ravi and his family went on a picnic. There was a race to the train. Guess who came last? Ravi.

Everyone else got a comfy seat, but Ravi had to squeeze in with Dad and Biscuits.

Then Biscuits made a bad smell.

When everyone got to the park,
they played **hide-and-seek**.

It was meant to be fun, but
Ravi couldn't find *anyone*.

At the playground, the monkey bars were too **high**.

The **gaps** between the logs were too **wide**.

And when Ravi wanted to **go** on
the BIG slide, the man said,
"Sorry, son, you're **too small**."

TALL TO SLIDE

Ravi got *so* mad
that his face turned red,
but then Dad said, "Come on,
let's get ice cream!"

Everybody ran off.
Guess who came last? Ravi.

And *then*, when Ravi went to
get *his* ice cream . . .

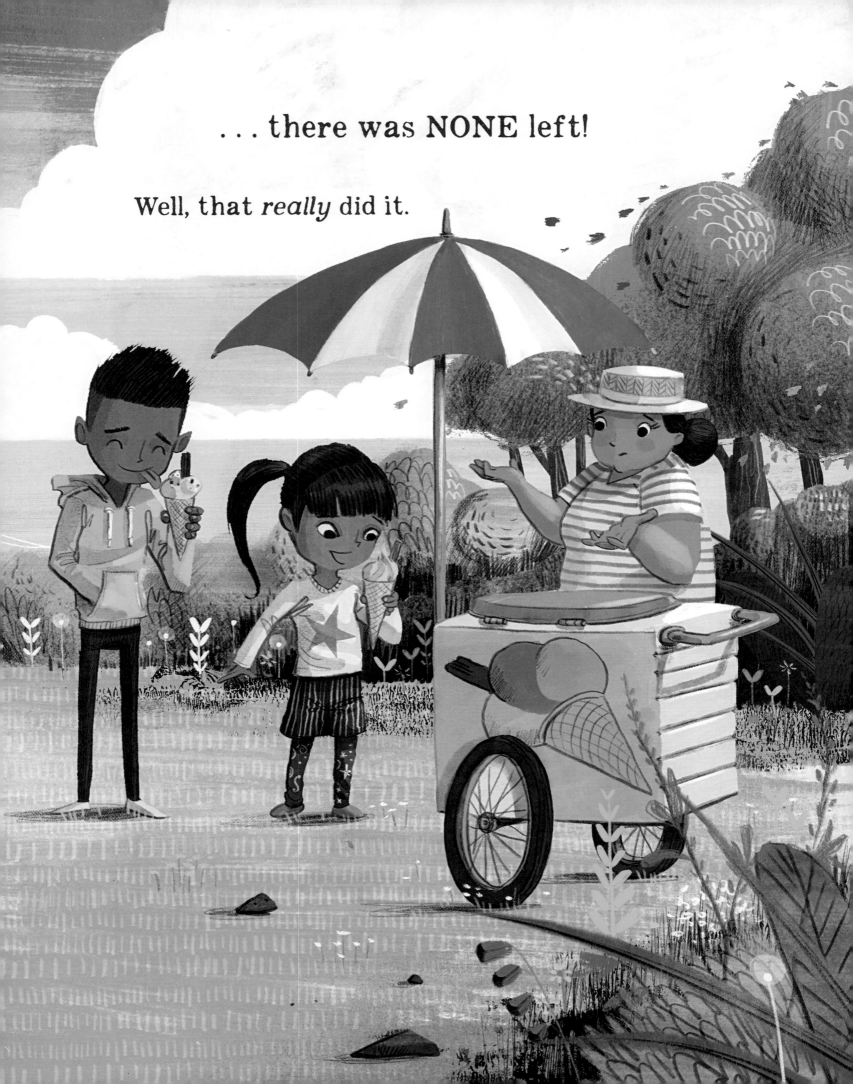

... there was NONE left!

Well, that *really* did it.

Ravi was FURIOUS!

He growled . . .

and **a stripy tail** popped out
from the back of his shorts.

Then . . .

he sprouted two **furry ears**,
sharp, **pointy teeth**,
and stripy **orange fur!**

Ravi had turned into a
TIGER!

The tiger took a **huge**,
deep breath, and then . . .

Ravi's brother looked a bit nervous
and handed the tiger his ice cream.

When the tiger went to sit down there were
no open benches, so he ROARED . . .

and *everybody* got out of the way.

It was GREAT
being a tiger!

The tiger did *all* the things that Ravi couldn't.

He swung across the monkey bars.
He leaped across the logs.

He even
slid down
the
BIG
slide!

Nobody dared
to say NO . . .

So the tiger went

WILD!

He roared and growled
and did *exactly* what
he wanted.

ROAR!

But soon he found that *nobody*
wanted to play with him.

Suddenly the tiger felt a bit sad
and nowhere near as angry.

In fact, he couldn't *quite* remember what
had made him so angry in the first place.

"I'm sorry . . . ," said the tiger in a quiet voice, and when he said that, *everything* felt better.

"That's okay," said Dad. "Good job for saying sorry!"

Then, without even realizing,
Ravi became a **boy** once more.

And that was the last time that
Ravi ever turned into a tiger.

Although every
now and then . . .

he did have a *bit* of a growl!

Dear Reader,

This is a book about a boy who has a bad day and is angry about it. Everybody gets mad sometimes, for a lot of different reasons—and that's okay. We all have LOTS of different feelings, and we use these feelings to help us understand the world. But it doesn't feel good to get *TOO* angry, and sometimes it causes us to be not nice to other people. So whenever you're mad, here are a few questions to ask yourself:

- ➤ What happened that is making me feel angry? Is it one thing, or a few different things?
- ➤ Is there anything I can do about it?
- ➤ If not, is there anyone I can talk to?
- ➤ Do I need to apologize to anyone I might have lashed out at?

No matter what you're feeling, remember that it always helps to talk about it. Be open, be honest, be YOU!

Love,

TOM

Here's an organization that offers resources if you're interested in learning more: **childmind.org**

5